CLIFFHANGERS

The most exciting books you've ever read!

by
Eric Weiner

RUNAWAY BUS!

Freddy is always late for school. But today, it's not his fault—he's chasing bank robbers in a school bus with no brakes!

DON'T LOOK DOWN!

Taking care of her neighbor's cat is a real easy job for Denise. But she didn't know she'd have to walk out on a thirteenth-floor ledge to do it!

THRILL RIDE!

Only one thing scares Annie more than riding the huge roller coaster, the Serpent . . . getting stuck upside down on the biggest loop!

Collect them all...
IF YOU DARE!

AND DON'T EVEN
TRY TO PUT THEM DOWN!

ERIC WEINER

BERKLEY BOOKS, NEW YORK

DON'T LOOK DOWN!

A Berkley Book / published by arrangement with
the author

PRINTING HISTORY
Berkley edition / September 1996

The Putnam Berkley World Wide Web site address is
http://www.berkley.com

ISBN: 0-425-15415-7

BERKLEY®
Berkley Books are published by The Berkley Publishing Group,
200 Madison Avenue, New York, New York 10016.
BERKLEY and the "B" design
are trademarks belonging to Berkley Publishing Corporation.

PRINTED IN THE UNITED STATES OF AMERICA

10 9 8 7 6 5 4 3 2 1

CHAPTER 1

"**H**EY, DENISE," SAYS MY BROTHER CHARLIE, "did you know there are pigeons on the moon?"

"Pigeons on the moon? Who told you that?"

Charlie takes a giant step over a crack in the sidewalk. "Bobby."

I should have known.

Bobby is this truly annoying kid who lives on the thirteenth floor of our apartment building and is always filling Charlie's head with all kinds of nonsense.

"It's not true," I say. "There's no air on the moon. Nothing lives up there. And pigeons could never fly up there anyway."

"Bobby says."

I give Charlie a look. "It's not true."

"It is," Charlie insists.

Charlie's only six. I'm thirteen. I was seven when Charlie was born. My parents both work full-time. So in some ways, I'm more like Charlie's mom than his older sister. That's why I feel like it's part of my job to make sure he doesn't believe all the nutty stuff kids spew out.

I mean, what if Bobby or some other creep tells Charlie he can flap his arms and fly off the top of our building? What then?

I shudder at the thought. 'Cause right away I see Charlie flying end over end until—

Oh, thank you, brain. Thank you for giving me that horrible, horrible picture!

This is a problem I have. If I see a crack in the sidewalk, right away I imagine Charlie tripping over it and—

In the distance, a siren wails.

Hmm . . .

That's the third siren I've heard in the last few minutes. Must be a big fire somewhere.

I don't have to tell you what nightmare scene just popped into my head.

It's Tuesday. I'm walking Charlie home from school like I do every day. Charlie goes to first grade at the Sandor Fritz School for the Humanities on Seventy-first and Amsterdam. I'm in seventh grade at the Parker School for Girls on Eighty-ninth. To pick up Charlie, I have to miss the last study hall (excellent!) and hop in a cab. That's expensive. But it saves Mom or Dad from taking off from work.

Charlie and I used to have a routine. We'd walk up Amsterdam Avenue, stop to buy a big soft pretzel from the hot-dog vendor, then go right to the playground. I don't let Charlie do that anymore. Don't ask me why. It's because of this thing that happened at the playground last year which I really don't want to get into, if you don't mind. I don't even want to think about—

AYYYYYYY!

I just thought about it. Like when is this bad memory going to go away?

I guess I might as well tell you and get it over with.

Last year when Charlie was only five and I was twelve I took him to this playground on Amsterdam Avenue and Seventy-seventh Street. Charlie was scared to go on the jungle gym. Well, I didn't want Charlie to be scared. I wanted him to be fearless, like I was. So I took him all the way to the tippy-top of the big metal dome.

"See," I said, "there's nothing to be scared of." Then I raised my arms in triumph.

Charlie copied me. And fell. Down to his death. At least, that's what I thought. Because he just lay there, facedown, not moving. I could see the back of his head, that wavy red hair.

It was the single worst moment of my life. I felt like someone had blown my head off.

You probably think I'm exaggerating. But seeing Charlie lying there?

The thing is, the playground has thick rubber mats so that kids don't destroy themselves when they fall. Charlie was scared and banged up and he cried a lot, but mostly, he was fine.

I wasn't.

Ever since then I've had this fear of heights like you would not believe.

To avoid passing the playground, I walk Charlie up Broadway, which is where we are now. On a warm spring day like this, Broadway is a great place. Everyone in New York City comes outside.

There are shoppers, people out for a stroll, old ladies squeezing the cantaloupes outside the open fruit markets, homeless people asking for money, volunteers trying to get you to sign petitions, a guy playing the violin really badly hoping people will tip him, messengers carrying packages on bikes, people walking their dogs, Roller Bladers, and a girl in a chicken suit who hands out green discount coupons for spicy wings at Chickie's.

Almost everyone seems to be in a great mood, too, 'cause of the sunshine and the—

A big red fire engine screams down the street, lights flashing, siren blasting. I can see all the firemen in their black-and-yellow raincoats hanging off the truck. They look angry, serious. Cars and taxis slowly move over to the side of the road to let the engine pass.

"Come on, Denise!" Charlie pulls on my hand. "Let's chase the truck and find the fire!"

"Let's not and say we did."

The truck passes. The siren fades. My heartbeat slows back to normal.

We reach the corner of Seventy-eighth Street. There are no cars coming. But even though there are plenty of people crossing, I hold Charlie back by his purple L.L. Bean backpack until the light changes.

Charlie's backpack is monogrammed with his initials, C.R.A.—Charles Robert Alexander. It's also decorated (by me) with all these safety reflector strips. Charlie lowers his head and growls as he strains against the backpack like a dog on a leash. I can't help laughing. When the light changes to WALK, I let him pull me off the sidewalk.

But I'm thinking about the fire truck.

At night Charlie likes me to read him a scary story, anything with ghosts or goblins or witches or imps. Maybe he likes those creepy stories because deep down he knows they're made up and silly.

But that fire truck—

That fire truck is on its way to a real emergency. Real danger. A place where bad things happen and there isn't always a happy ending. A place where Charlie could—

"You know how I know there are no pigeons on the moon?" I ask Charlie suddenly, forcing a grin.

Charlie stops short. "How?"

" 'Cause I rode up to the moon in my rocket ship and checked."

Charlie's jaw drops. He's standing in the middle of Seventy-eighth Street. I tug on his hand but he yanks it free. "For real?" he asks.

Charlie's going through this phase where he believes everything you tell him unless you say it's not for real.

"No, not for real," I say. I give him a look. "But you knew that, right, Charlie? So why'd you have to ask?"

I tug on Charlie's hand. "Come on!"

But he squats down to pick up a piece of green paper.

Charlie's always thinking he's found money. This is just one of those discount Chickie's coupons. Everyone who takes a coupon tosses it by the next block. So on Seventy-eighth there are green slips everywhere.

"Charlie! Let's go!" I say, my voice rising. "We're in the middle of the—"

I freeze as the—

Ambulance swerves around the corner, headed right at us!

CHAPTER 2

THERE ARE SHOUTS.

Heads turn.

I yank Charlie's arm so hard I lift him into the air. I pull him out of the way of the ambulance, which comes so close to hitting us I feel like a matador waving a red flag in front of a bull.

We stare at the ambulance as it roars away, siren screaming.

"Stupid ambulance!" snarls a man standing next to us, shaking his head. "How many people are they going to hit on the way to the accident!"

I'm shaking. I carry Charlie out of the street.

"You okay?" a woman with her arms full of packages stops to ask us.

"Yeah, thanks," I mumble.

People always say New Yorkers are rude. I think

that's rude to say that. Anyway, it's not true. Lots of
New Yorkers are friendly and nice.

Charlie, by the way, is fine. Me—

I'm holding Charlie with one hand—tight—but
I've got my eyes closed so I don't throw up.

That . . . was . . . close.

When I open my eyes, Charlie's mouth is open,
and he's pointing down Seventy-eighth, where the
ambulance and the fire truck both went.

He's right. The fire truck and the ambulance are
both headed where we're headed. Toward West End
Avenue.

Toward home.

"Come on, Denise," yells Charlie. "Maybe our
building is on fire!"

Great.

I keep one hand tight on Charlie's shoulder so he
doesn't get too far ahead of me as we both jog down
the sidewalk toward—

Uh-oh.

There's this big crowd gathered at the end of the
block. Unless there's a street fair, the only reason
people block traffic like this is if there's been a
terrible accident or crime.

"Awesome," gushes Charlie as we come closer.

That's a word he picked up from Bobby. But he's
right. It's awesome.

There are cops everywhere. There are parked
patrol cars, doors open, lights flashing. The cops
have put out blue sawhorses stopping traffic from
Seventy-seventh to Seventy-eighth.

Charlie taps people on the back and yells,

"What's going on? What's going on?" He jumps up, trying to get a look.

Charlie's short for his age. Me, I've been sprouting. I'm built like a stick pretty much. So I can see there's this huge blue thing, looks like a giant marshmallow, which the firemen have set up on the sidewalk.

Why?

I start chewing on my bead necklace, which I always do when I'm nervous. Then some old man with a cane hobbles over and takes my arm. "Car crash?" he asks me. All eager, too. Like a good car crash would really make his day.

"I don't know," I say, my mouth going dry. "I just got here."

"It's a jumper," someone tells the old man, and points.

Up.

You know how some people have a fear of heights? And when they're up high they're so scared that they can't look down?

Well I have it worse than that.

I can't even look up at someplace high when I'm down on the ground. It makes me sick.

Don't look, I tell myself.

Don't look, Denise, and maybe you won't puke or faint or—

I look.

And sure enough. There's a man standing on the roof of Hamilton House.

Hamilton House is an old apartment building. It's fourteen stories high, just like the Westholme, the building where Charlie and I live.

Fourteen stories—that's high. Standing on the roof, this man seems so tiny he looks like a toy.

The big bright sun sits right behind him, making him into a tiny silhouette. I have to pull down the visor of my Yankees cap and squint hard to see him.

He's looking down at us. He's got his gray suit jacket slung over one shoulder like he's waiting for a bus instead of waiting to die.

I can't tell you how weird it feels, seeing this guy up there. How weird and awful.

I've lived in New York City my whole life. People who don't live here, they read about all the scary crime that happens in New York City and they think it's a bad place.

It's not like that. At least not where I live. I mean, I've almost never had any trouble. And now suddenly—it's like I'm in the middle of the five o'clock news.

In fact, there's the big yellow Channel 7 news van with a satellite dish right on top.

"If he's going to jump, I wish he'd jump already," jokes the woman next to me. "I've got a lot of errands to run."

All around us people laugh, which makes me feel even sicker. I can't watch anymore. I just can't. So I look down.

And there's Charlie.

He's got his head all the way back and his mouth so wide open it's like he's planning on swallowing the man when he falls. He's got his little hands shoved deep in the pockets of his khaki shorts.

My brother Charlie is a pretty cute kid, I gotta say, and not just 'cause he's my brother. He has red hair, a little button nose, and the most amazing green eyes you ever saw. And right now those eyes have this look Charlie gets when he's watching something on TV that he's not supposed to watch. Something on Pay-Per-View, for instance.

I can't believe I'm letting him see something so scary and so grisly.

"Come on," I tell him, "we're out of here."

I pull his hand out of his pocket and yank on it, but my hand has gone all sweaty and Charlie has no problem pulling his hand out of mine. "Denise?" he asks, frowning. "What's wrong with that guy? Why does he want to jump?"

"I don't know. I guess he's crazy. C'mon, Charlie, I mean it. Let's—"

Suddenly the crowd screams.

"DENISE!" Charlie yells, pointing up. "HE'S FALLING!"

CHAPTER 3

THE MAN TUMBLES END OVER END, EXCEPT—

It's not the guy! It's just his suit jacket. He must have dropped it.

Yes!

The jacket sails down, down, down until it thwacks onto a manhole in the middle of the street.

I start breathing again. There's an "Oooh" of relief from the crowd. Some kids race over and fight over who's going to get the man's jacket, like it's a baseball that Ken Griffey, Jr., just slugged into the bleachers.

Then someone yells up at the man, "You dropped your jacket!" and everyone laughs.

Once, on the TV news, I heard about a man in midtown who stood on a window ledge for hours. After a while the crowd started yelling for the guy to jump. Hearing everyone laugh like this, I can believe it. It makes me mad.

"Charlie," I say firmly, "we're going home. Now."

Charlie looks at me like I'm from another planet. "I don't want to go home. I want to—"

"Now," I say.

I get a good grip on Charlie's neck and march him through the crowd.

"Deniiise—don't you want to—*ow!*—don't you want to see if—"

"No! Move it!"

Once we make it out of the cluster of spectators, I steer Charlie to the sidewalk. He keeps twisting away so he can look back at the top of Hamilton House. My whole body is tense, waiting for the scream from the crowd when the man really jumps.

And the thud.

It's like I'm waiting to get shot in the back.

Even though it's only two buildings away, I feel a little better once we get to the big red awning of our building, the Westholme. Home sweet home.

There's a big moving van parked out front. M&M Movers. Then I spot Mrs. Carmen, the old lady who always sits out front in a folding lawn chair, people-watching. And there's Fernando, our doorman, who gives me a big smile.

"Denise and Charlie!" Fernando says in his heavy Spanish accent.

Fernando is from Venezuela. He doesn't speak much English. Whenever he sees us, he says our names just like this. "Denise and Charlie!" I don't know why, but it's like this running joke between us. It always makes me feel good.

"Fernando, there's a guy up on the roof!" Charlie squeals. "Do you see him? He's going to jump! Can you believe it! Look! There! Do you see him?"

Fernando lets Charlie hang off his hand like his arm is a rope, but he doesn't budge from his post. "I know," he says seriously. "Very bad."

Fernando looks at me. He doesn't say anything but I can tell by his look what he's saying. *Get Charlie inside.*

I'm trying, I answer back with my eyes.

"Poor Mr. Slocum," says old Mrs. Carmen, clucking her tongue. "He misses his kids so bad."

"You know him?" Charlie asks, letting go of Fernando and running over to Mrs. Carmen.

Mrs. Carmen knows everything about everybody in our building and on our block, just about. She ought to. She's retired, and when it's nice weather she sits out here for hours.

"Sure I know him," she says, brushing some crumbs from her faded house dress. "He's divorced. Three children." She holds up three fingers. "But his ex-wife won't let him see the kids." She makes a face. "Poor Mr. Slocum. He's always telling me how sad he is. Now this. Ugh. I see it coming. I see it coming."

My body tenses up all over again. It makes the whole thing seem so much more real, now that I know somebody who knows the guy on the roof.

Please come down, I pray. Please don't jump.

"He's going to jump," Mrs. Carmen says, "I promise you."

"Come on, Charlie," I say, "let's go inside. We've got to see Fluffy. Fluffy's lonely, Charlie. Please."

Fluffy is a cat. Our neighbor, Ms. Orson, pays me and Charlie four dollars a day to play with her after school. It's a really easy job. We don't have to change her kitty litter or anything, just hang out with her so she's not so lonely.

I like playing with Fluffy, but right now, as you probably guessed, I'm just using her as an excuse.

Unfortunately, Charlie probably guessed, too. "Do *you* think he's going to jump?" he asks Fernando, ignoring me. "Do you?"

"Watch out," Fernando tells him as a moving man rolls one end of a large sofa on a dolly through the open lobby doors.

There are three moving men. They all stop when they reach the sidewalk, obviously upset to see the street roped off.

"What's going on?" one of the movers asks.

"There's a jumper!" Charlie gasps, excited to have someone new to tell. "Look!"

"How are we going to get our truck out of here?" the mover asks Fernando, who shrugs.

Nice. A man might jump off a building, all these movers care about is running a little behind schedule.

I guide Charlie into the big lobby. Once we're inside, I breathe a big sigh of relief. In here, the sound of the mob out on the street is a lot quieter.

The lobby of the Westholme is like a cavern, with a high ceiling, marble floors, fake potted palms, shiny brass mailboxes, and leather sofas.

I don't want you to think I'm rich or something. I'm not. Wait till you see the inside of my apartment. It's a real dump.

See, we're renters. The Westholme went co-op a few years ago. That means a lot of rich people bought apartments in the building and fixed up the apartments and the lobby all fancy.

But the rest of the people who live here are people who've been living here for ages. Renters like Mrs. Carmen and Charlie and Mom and Dad and me. You can tell because we've got the apartments with the peeling paint and the uneven floors.

Once Charlie and I are inside our apartment, I breathe another deep sigh of relief. Because I got Charlie home safe. I got him out of that horrible scene that's happening right on our street.

You know, sometimes I can't believe Mom still trusts me to take care of Charlie, after what happened at the playground.

I was so lucky that he was okay.

What if I'm not that lucky the next time?

There can't be a next time, that's all.

Our apartment smells dusty. I can hear the fridge humming in the kitchen. Our apartment faces the street. And as I take off my backpack in the living room, Charlie runs to the window to see if he can see the man on the roof.

When he opens the window I can hear the crowd yelling. Not a sound I want to hear right now.

Charlie sticks his head outside.

"Hey, careful!" I say.

I watch him closely, ready to run across the room and dive and grab him if he leans out any farther.

Finally, Charlie sticks his head back inside, frowning at me. "I can't see him."

That's a relief.

"Close the window, would ya?" I ask.

He doesn't. "Hey, Denise," he says, his eyes sparkling with a new idea, "know what we can play? Man on the Roof."

I don't have to ask how you play. "No way," I say. "Come on, Charlie. Close the window."

Charlie stamps his foot, his face red and angry. "Denise! Just once!"

Mom says I spoil Charlie and give in to everything he asks. Well, I'm not going to give in and play Man on the Roof, that's for sure.

"No. You want some cookies? There are some Mint Choco-bars in the fridge."

"I hate Mint Choco-bars."

This is a lie. True, Charlie likes some cookies better than others (his favorite is gingersnaps), but he has never met a cookie he didn't like. Not that he ever gains an ounce.

"Let's see what else there is," I say, wandering into the kitchen. I flick on the lights. I can feel these big wet spots on my back where the straps of my backpack used to be. Sweat.

I like to think of myself as this real street-smart, tough New Yorker. But that's when I'm by myself. When I'm watching over Charlie, I'm a wreck. And anyway, that guy on the roof really freaked me out. I mean, wouldn't you get upset if you saw a guy getting ready to kill himself?

I open the cupboard. Awesome—as Charlie and Bobby would say. Mom bought more gingersnaps. That ought to make my brother happy.

"Yo, Charles," I say, coming back into the living

room. "I've got some excellent news for you. What's your favorite—"

But Charlie isn't in the living room.

I shut the window. Lock it.

"Hey, Charlie," I say, heading down the hall, flicking on lights as I go, "guess what Mom bought you?"

No answer.

The door to Charlie's room is open. I stick my head inside. Except he's not in here either.

I'm about to move on down the hall when I see that Charlie has opened the window in his room.

And then my heart starts to beat so hard it's like I swallowed a pigeon.

Because there's Charlie.

Out on the ledge.

CHAPTER 4

"CHARLIE!" I SHRIEK.

Standing out on the narrow ledge, Charlie slowly turns and looks at me.

He grins.

Waves.

"I'm playing Man on the Roof," he calls.

Then he turns back to the street.

And jumps—

CHAPTER 5

THREE FEET DOWN TO THE GARDEN BELOW.

I guess I didn't mention that we live on the first floor.

Well, we do. Apartment 1-B.

I run to the window to make sure Charlie didn't hurt himself falling into the bushes.

He's fine.

I used to hate living on the first floor. People say that burglars love to pick on ground-floor apartments, since they can climb in through the windows.

We have a doorman to protect us, but last month there was a robbery in the building. Three men pretended they were painting Apartment 2-C and made off with all this jewelry.

That scared me plenty. But I'm still glad we live

on the first floor. It's 'cause of my wicked fear of heights. I mean, these days I can't even handle Charlie *pretending* to be out on the ledge, only three feet up.

Fernando gives Charlie a boost back into the window. "I don't like this game so much," Fernando tells him gently.

"You hear that?" I tell Charlie as I help him back inside. "You got Fernando really furious."

Which is, of course, not true. I've never seen Fernando mad in my life. It's me who's shaking.

Outside, another siren wails. I can see the three movers wrestling a large old wooden wardrobe up onto their truck. They're working hard and fast. I shut Charlie's window and lock it.

Then I look at Charlie.

I guess I give him a pretty mean look because he blushes. "Sorry," he says. "I was just goofing." He looks sorry, too.

Which is enough to make me forgive him.

While Charlie sits at the kitchen table eating gingersnaps and drinking milk, I call Mom at her office, which I do every day just to let her know we got home safe. It's silly, I guess. Because if we *didn't* call it would probably mean it was too late for Mom to do anything to help us. But I always feel better after I talk to her.

"Let me talk!" Charlie cries. "Let me talk!"

I'm about to hand him the phone, but then I hear Mom talking to someone. One of her bosses, I guess. "I'll call you back in a minute," she tells me. Then she hangs up.

Mom's always busy at work. She's an actress, but

not like a movie star or anything. In fact, she almost never gets an audition. While she's waiting for her big break she works as a word processor for all these lawyers. The lawyers don't like it when she makes personal calls. And sometimes when she has to hang up, she doesn't even have time to say good-bye.

"Why didn't you let me talk to her?" Charlie demands.

"She had to go. She'll call back."

Charlie drops a cookie back on the table.

"She'll call back," I repeat.

Charlie rubs his cheek with the heel of his hand, smearing his face with ginger crumbs. "You didn't tell her about the guy on the roof," he says, his teeth orange with cookie mush.

"I know."

I rummage around the kitchen drawer next to the sink until I find the key to Ms. Orson's apartment.

"How come?" Charlie demands.

"Because she'd freak out and leave work and come home to be with us and we're broke enough as it is. And don't open your mouth while you eat, it's disgusting. Come on. Let's go play with Fluffy."

"Seafood, seafood," Charlie chants, grinning at me, his mouth open wide.

"Funny." I smile and run my hand through Charlie's hair.

"Cut it out," he says, shaking his head.

"Sorry."

He hates it when I tousle his hair like this, but I can't help it. Charlie's got these soft, wavy red locks.

Me, I've got hair the same red color but it's in tight little curls. My hair looks like a big bowl of burned pasta noodles that somebody dumped on my head. Which is why I always wear my Yankees cap, if you want to know the truth.

"Come on," I tell Charlie, tipping him out of his chair.

"You want an ABC cookie?" Charlie asks me as we head for the front door.

"Ooo, that joke's so old it ought to be in an old-age home," I tell him.

He looks surprised. "You know what ABC means?"

"Already Been Chewed."

His jaw drops. "Who told you?"

"Fluffy told me," I say.

"Fluffy? Fluffy the cat told you the ABC joke? For real?"

"No, not for real."

Out in the hall, I kneel down and tie Charlie's shoelaces, which I'm sure will stay tied for about five seconds.

"Stop," he says, trying to pull his shoe away.

"*You* stop," I tell him. I pull his sneaker back toward me.

"Denise—it's the way kids wear them. You know. Cool kids."

"Who told you that?"

"Bobby."

I roll my eyes. See? What did I tell you?

"You won't look cool when you trip and fall, believe me," I tell Charlie as I unlock our front door.

I'm about to close the door behind us, but first I

check to make sure I've got our key in my pocket so I don't lock us out.

Fernando keeps spare keys to all the apartments in the doorman's coat closet. But Charlie locks himself out so often that sometimes he locks all the spare keys inside the apartment along with his regular key, so I really have to be careful.

I shut and lock our door, 1-B. Then we pad across the lobby's marble floor to Ms. Orson's apartment, 1-A.

"Denise and Charlie!" calls Fernando from his desk.

Charlie and I both wave.

We have three locks on our door. Ms. Orson has *four*. I'm right in the middle of opening the last lock when I get this awful creepy feeling. Something's wrong.

"What?" Charlie asks, looking at me.

Ms. Orson is away all day working. By the afternoon, Fluffy gets really lonely. So when we come over, she's always waiting right at the door for us, meowing and scratching.

Only now . . .

Apartment 1-A sounds totally quiet.

Fluffy's not at the door.

Okay. So maybe today she's *so* lonely that she's waiting silently.

"What?" Charlie says again.

I look at him blankly. Then I shove open the door.

Fluffy is a white Persian. She's old, but she can still scoot. To be safe, I only open the door a little bit. Charlie kneels down, peering through the crack in the door into the dark apartment. Then he looks up at me, puzzled.

"She's not here," he says.

I shrug. "She's inside."

Which is not what I'm thinking, of course. I'm thinking something awful. Fluffy is old. What if she died?

That would be the worst. Ms. Orson is divorced. She doesn't have kids. All she has is Fluffy. If something happened to Fluffy, she'd be all alone.

"Okay," I say, trying to stay calm. "We go in fast. Then I shut the door. Got it?"

Charlie nods. "Got it."

My plan works. Except for one thing. I forgot about the light. So when I slam the door behind us, we're in the pitch dark.

"Fluffy?" I call.

No meow. No little pitty-pat of cat paws on the hardwood floor. I fumble for the light switch. Only before I can reach it, my hand freezes along the wall because—

Am I crazy or did I just hear footsteps?

I'm crazy, right?

"Denise?" Charlie asks, his voice soft and faint. "Did you hear that?"

You know what? I'm not crazy. Because there it is again. Yup. Definitely footsteps. And not little cat footsteps, either. Big human footsteps!

Charlie clutches my T-shirt in the dark as—

The robber steps out through the swinging doors of the kitchen.

He's pointing his gun right at us!

CHAPTER 6

I FLING OPEN THE FRONT DOOR SO WE CAN RUN OUT into the lobby and get Fernando.

"Bang bang, you're dead," says the robber.

It's a familiar voice, high and squeaky.

I turn around slowly.

Sure enough, there stands Bobby Lawrence, pointing his finger at us. No gun at all.

I flick on the lights. Bobby blows imaginary smoke from his stubby finger. "Gotcha," he says proudly.

Bobby Lawrence lives in 13-D. He's rich and twelve and fat. He looks like a huge serving of mashed potatoes.

Bobby's parents are both movie producers who are always flying out to Hollywood. I don't know them. But I know Bobby. Bobby has almost no friends and spends all his time hanging out in the lobby bothering Fernando or trying to think of dumb practical jokes to play on the tenants. Like one time he came over to visit us and hid a plastic rat behind our cereal boxes so that when Dad went to get his cereal for breakfast he practically had a seizure.

But you know what? I probably wouldn't mind Bobby so much if Charlie didn't like him so much.

Charlie races over to him. "Bobby! Bobby! Did you see him? Did you see the guy? The guy on the roof?"

"Are you kidding?" asks Bobby. "Who do you think called the cops?"

"Who?" asks Charlie.

Bobby pats his chest.

"For real?"

"For bull-twinkie," I say as I hurry down the hallway toward Ms. Orson's bedroom. "Fluffy?" I call. "Fluffy! Fluffy!"

Now that I'm over my terror of a robbery in progress in Ms. Orson's apartment, I'm back to worrying about Fluffy.

I don't have to worry. Fluffy's curled up on the bed, half-asleep. She opens one gray eye and looks at me.

"Fluffy? You okay? You're not sick, are you?" I plop down on the bed and start stroking her from her head down her back. Fluffy purrs like a little motorboat, lifting her head to meet my hand with each stroke.

"You scared me," I tell her.

Fluffy gets up, stretches her whole body, then starts licking off her paws.

Ms. Orson keeps her place really neat. Everything she owns is old and made out of wood. It's sort of a like an antique store. In her bedroom, she's got these old opera posters all over the walls. Also photos of Ms. Orson in various costumes, singing in these different operas that she was in when she was in college.

Ms. Orson is a renter like us. She wants to be an opera star someday, but right now she works as a secretary.

Ms. Orson is one of Mom's best friends. She's tall, black, and very skinny. Ms. Orson says that opera singers don't have to be fat, which I never knew. It's true, too. You should hear Ms. Orson practice at night. She sounds just as good as the opera singers on the radio.

"Fluffy's okay," I tell one of Ms. Orson's photos on the wall. I feel very very relieved.

Bobby fills the doorway.

"You're an idiot," I tell him, petting Fluffy and not looking at him.

"I've been playing with her for like twenty minutes," Bobby says.

No wonder she wasn't at the door. Twenty minutes with Bobby is enough to make anyone hide in the bedroom.

"Where were you guys, anyway?" Bobby asks.

Which reminds me.

"How did you get in here?" I demand.

Bobby grins proudly. "Spare key in the doorman's coat closet."

"You *stole* it?" Charlie asks him.

"Piece of cake," boasts Bobby.

Great thinking, Bobby Lawrence. Like stealing is really what I want to teach Charlie. "He probably lied to Fernando," I tell Charlie, "and said he locked himself out of his apartment. It's not hard to steal, Charlie, it's just bad." I glare at Bobby. "Listen, you have no right to be in here. You know that, don't you? I'm going to tell Ms. Orson."

Bobby grins like I just paid him a huge compliment. "Go ahead and tell her. Ms. Orson likes me just as much as you."

"Yeah? Well that doesn't mean she wants you in her apartment when she's not home."

"She lets *you* come in."

"We're working for her. It's a job."

"So maybe I'll ask her if she'll hire me, too."

I can feel my blood starting to boil. I try to tell myself to stay calm. A lot of good that does me.

"You should have seen the look on your face," taunts Bobby. He imitates me, shaking and shivering. "Oh, no, it's a robber! It's a robber!"

I didn't say any of that. I didn't say a word, in fact. But he's right. That's just what I was thinking.

Charlie giggles. "I almost peed in my pants," he tells Bobby. Then he roars happily and runs straight at Bobby, trying to butt him in his big belly with his head.

"Incoming!" Bobby shouts, grabbing Charlie in a headlock.

This is some crazy game they always play. I never quite get it. Sometimes it has to do with war movies and sometimes it has to do with pro wrestling.

"Watch out!" I yell.

Too late.

There's a crash as they bang into this fancy old mirror on the wall. It's the kind of mirror that has little worm holes in its wooden frame. Probably costs a fortune. And Bobby and Charlie came *this* close to knocking it off the wall.

"That was close," Bobby says, looking nervous. Then he grins and yells, "Bruno the Beast grabs little Tony in a death grip!"

He gets Charlie around the middle, lifting him off the floor. I hear a plop from behind me.

Fluffy jumped off the bed. She stretches once, yawns, then scoots for the door.

Which is when I remember.

I left the front door of the apartment open.

I fall to my knees trying to catch Fluffy but she jumps right through my arms. I scramble back up and run into the hall. I probably shouldn't be running because I'm chasing Fluffy and that's making her run faster. She races into the living room and—

I don't believe it.

She just ran right out the door.

Well, what am I doing? I'm just standing here, staring at the open door, that's what I'm doing. And meanwhile Fluffy's out in the lobby. She could run out into the street! She could get hit by a—

I start running again, barreling out into the lobby with Bobby and Charlie right behind me.

Then I stop short. Bobby and Charlie bash into me from behind.

The reason I stopped short?

I can see Fluffy's fluffy white tail disappearing onto the elevator. The elevator doors are closing, too. I hold my breath as the doors almost, but not quite, nip Fluffy's tail.

The little metal arrow above the elevator starts rising, rising.

Unbelievable.

Fluffy's on the elevator.

And the elevator is going up.

CHAPTER 7

I STARE AT THE ARROW, STUNNED.

2 . . . 3 . . . 4 . . .

The arrow stops. It points to "6." And stays there.

I couldn't be more shocked if Fluffy went out in the street and hailed a taxi.

"Wow, Charlie," Bobby murmurs. "Did you see that? Fluffy just took the elevator to the sixth floor."

"For *real*?"

"No," I tell Charlie quickly. "Someone must have called the elevator to the sixth floor."

Whoever it is, they're in for a little surprise.

"Well, I'm out of here," Bobby says happily.

Like this isn't his problem. Like he had nothing to do with it. I stare at him, furious, trying to melt him into a puddle with my eyes.

"Don't look at *me*," he says. "I'm not the one who left the door open."

I want to pummel him. I want to get him in one of those death grips of his.

"Anyway, what's the big deal?" says Bobby. "Where's she going to go? You'll get her. Don't sweat it."

I force myself to look away from Bobby. I also force myself not to call him Blobby. A kid on the playground over at Seventy-seventh and Amsterdam once called him that over and over until he burst into tears.

I guess I could wait for the elevator to come back down. But I can't stand waiting.

"Charlie," I say, "close Ms. Orson's door. Now."

Charlie runs and slams the door. There's a latch on the door that locks when you close it. I don't have time to bother with the other locks now.

Bobby yawns. "I'm going to the grocery, get a snacky-poo. You want anything, Chuck?"

He doesn't ask me if *I* want anything, you notice. And he calls Charlie a nickname I despise. Charlie asks for cinnamon gum, which Bobby promises to buy him. Then he strolls out of the lobby, slapping Fernando on the back like Fernando is a kid Bobby's age.

But I don't have time to deal with Bobby now. Fluffy's on the sixth floor. I start to run for the stairs, pulling Charlie along with me. Then I stop short. I have a better idea. I hiss at Charlie, "The service elevator!"

"The service elevator!" Charlie yells back.

The service elevator is this old beat-up elevator

that doesn't have a security camera like the main elevator does. It also doesn't have an automatically closing door. Instead it's got this metal gate that you close yourself. And there's this big metal lever that runs the service elevator up and down.

You're not supposed to use the service elevator. It's only for workmen or the handyman or movers. But this is an emergency.

Right now the service elevator is loaded with chairs and a lamp and boxes and stuff marked R&R MOVERS. I have to move a seat cushion out of the way to get to the lever.

"Let me run it," Charlie begs me. "Puh-lease!"

"No. Watch out."

I push Charlie's hand away from the big lever. "I said watch it." Then I pull the lever to GO.

Only the elevator doesn't move an inch.

I stare at the lever. Now what?

"You have to close the metal gate," Charlie tells me. "Or else it won't go."

He doesn't say it meanly, either. Good old Charlie. How many kids could resist rubbing it in when their older sister made such a stupid mistake? Especially after I just told him he couldn't run the elevator.

I smile. I've got sweat all over my face. "Right," I say.

Please be okay, Fluffy. Please be okay.

I reach for the handle that shuts the metal gate. But before I reach the handle—

A large angry face shoves itself right into mine!

CHAPTER 8

"**W**HAT DO YOU THINK YOU'RE DOING?" THIS MAN growls at me. He's red in the face like he's going to pop a vein.

I back away, or try to, but in the crowded elevator I step on all these boxes and almost go down.

The man who's glaring at me is short. He wears a leather weight-lifting belt and a white shirt with the arms cut off and tattoos all over his bulging biceps. PETE, say the letters sewn in script across the breast pocket of his shirt.

"I said what are you doing?" Pete barks at me.

Now I know who this is. One of the movers.

"We were just playing," Charlie says. He's trying to lead me off the service elevator and away from the angry mover.

"You see we're in the middle of moving here? You see that?"

"Yeah," I say. "But—our cat—"

Pete pokes his finger into my forehead, like he's pushing an elevator button. "You don't use the service. You get me? You do not use the service."

"Emergency," I stammer. I point up. "Our cat," I say.

"Yeah, she pushed the button on the elevator," Charlie explains.

Pete shakes his head, chuckling. But not friendly, more like he's going to kill us. "Your cat pushed the button on the elevator?"

"Uh-huh," says Charlie, then he adds, "For real."

"She's on the sixth floor," I explain.

"Okay," Pete says, "here's the deal. Sorry if I scared you, but I had to get your attention. And now that I've got your attention, let me make my point very clear. I don't care if your grandmother is on the moon. You do not play with this elevator. You get me?"

"I—get you."

I hate when grown-ups yell at kids. And of course I hate when they yell at me most of all. Don't you always get the feeling that they're taking all this stuff out on you that doesn't have anything to do with you?

Charlie's already back out in the lobby. "Denise," he calls, "the elevator is coming back down!"

"Excuse me," I say, stepping around Pete. I don't feel like I owe him any apology, that's for sure. Not after the way he just acted.

I hear the service elevator's metal gate screech

shut behind me. Pete rides off without another word.

I add Pete to my list of things I don't have time for right now. Right after Bobby. Because Charlie's right. The metal arrow over the main elevator is dropping, dropping. It drops down to "1." Here comes Fluffy.

Please. Fluffy. Be okay.

The doors glide open. And Charlie and I just stare.

Because there's no Fluffy on the elevator. Just our neighbor Mr. Loomis and his giant dog.

Mr. Loomis is a writer who Mrs. Carmen says has never sold a book but who lives off all this money he inherited. All I ever see him doing is going jogging with his huge Russian wolfhound, Boris.

As Mr. Loomis and his dog come off the elevator, Charlie runs into the elevator, then out again. "She's not on here!" Charlie yells to me. "Denise! Fluffy's gone!"

Gone?

I look at Mr. Loomis.

Then I look at Boris.

I thought I loved all animals. Then I met Boris. I mean, I don't know if you've ever seen a wolfhound. They're gigantic. Too big to be a pet, if you ask me. They're thin, too, with curved backs and thin faces. They give me the shakes. They look like monsters. And Boris is mean. He growls at everybody, tries to bite squirrels, the mail carriers, cats, and—

Cats?

Oh no . . .

Oh yes. As Boris trots into the lobby I get a close look at him. He's got these little white cat hairs all around his long thin snout.

And he's licking his chops.

CHAPTER 9

MY STOMACH GOES ALL WAVY LIKE I'M
going to chuck my cookies. What if Boris ate Fluffy?!

"Wait! Mr. Loomis!"

I run after him. Mr. Loomis pulls hard on Boris's
leash. Boris turns his thin head to stare at me,
growling low in his throat. Like Fluffy didn't fill up
that huge belly, and maybe I'm next.

"Easy, Boris," Mr. Loomis tells him.

The angry nasty way he yanks on Boris's leash
makes me think I know why Boris is so mean.

"Mr. Loomis!" I get as close as I can bear. I feel so
sick. "Did you see a cat—?" I gasp.

"A white cat," adds Charlie, coming up alongside
us.

I yank Charlie back so he doesn't get too close to

Boris. If Boris could swallow Fluffy, he could probably gulp down my little brother as well.

"Right," I say. "A white cat. On the elevator. Did you see her?"

Mr. Loomis jogs up and down in place, like he can't waste a moment of exercise. By the way, even though he's always jogging, he's got this big roll of fat around his middle. "Is that *your* cat?" he asks me. He sounds very annoyed.

"Yes!" I cry. "I mean, no. It's Ms. Orson's cat. But—"

"I was going to tell Fernando," says Mr. Loomis, jogging faster. He shakes his head at me, like he's very upset, and makes this tsk-tsk sound.

I can't take the suspense. "Tell Fernando what?!" I shriek, clutching my head with both hands.

Fernando comes running in from outside. Mr. Loomis looks at me very strangely. "Their cat came running off the elevator just as we were getting on," he tells Fernando. "Scared me half to death. It tried to scratch Boris, too."

Oh, I'm sure. I'm sure that's what happened.

"So she's on the sixth floor?" I ask quietly. Like if I say this loud I'll jinx myself.

"Yeah," says Mr. Loomis. "She's on the sixth floor."

"You need help?" Fernando asks me.

"Nah," I say. "We're okay."

Fernando goes back outside. I don't wait another second, just turn and run for the elevator.

But this bald neighbor of ours, I don't know his name, he gets there before us. And the doors close.

"Wait!" I yell.

"Wait!" shouts Charlie.

I can see our neighbor's big bald head, with the elevator lights shining off it. The man stares out at us, surprised, and reaches for the "Door Open" button. But he doesn't get to the button in time, because the doors shut and the metal arrow starts rising.

We can't take the service elevator, even if we wanted to risk another run-in with Pete. Because the service elevator is gone.

"Stairs," I tell Charlie, running so fast across the marble floor I slip and almost go down.

There are four stairways that run all the way up the four corners of the Westholme. The stairs take you in back of all the apartments. This is where everyone puts out their trash for the handyman, so it smells a little rotten on the stairs. And sometimes you see little roaches or big water bugs—

LIKE THAT ONE!

Oh, wow. A water bug the size of a cheeseburger just scurried past my feet.

As I guess you can tell, I'm not crazy about the stairs. But I don't have a choice.

I take the stairs two and three at a time. But then I have to slow down 'cause Charlie is getting too far behind. As much as I care about Fluffy, there's no way I'm leaving Charlie alone on the stairs. I wait for him. When he catches up, I see that his shoelaces have come untied—again. So I pick him up and start running.

Charlie yells at me to put him down, but I don't listen.

Second floor.

Now I listen. Because I'm gasping for breath. It's not so easy running up the stairs when you're carrying your younger brother.

So now we're both hurrying up the stairs.

Did I say hurrying? I think we're going slower now than if we had just walked the stairs in the first place. And every two seconds Charlie trips on his untied shoelaces.

But at least we keep going.

Third floor.

"We're—coming—Fluffy—!" I yell.

Like she can hear me.

Fourth floor.

Beth Cheever, this rich girl in my class? Her parents have a stair machine in their bedroom. I tried it once. After fifteen minutes the machine's message read, CONGRATULATIONS, YOU JUST CLIMBED 148 FLIGHTS OF STAIRS!

That machine must be busted, because I wasn't even out of breath. And right now I just climbed five real flights and I feel like I'm going to croak.

We trudge up the last flight. I have to stop outside the sixth-floor door for several seconds, gasping for breath. Then I yank open the door.

The sixth-floor hallway is lined with apartment doors. A big mirror and a side table face the elevators. One of the tenants has decorated the table with a vase of fake flowers. All the apartment doors are shut.

Fluffy is gone.

CHAPTER 10

CHARLIE AND I WANDER AROUND THE HALL-way like caged animals, trying all the doors.

Locked.

How could this be? What, Fluffy vanished into thin air?

Charlie's knocking on doors now, slapping them with the palm of his hand. "Open up!" he yells. "Police!"

"Charlie, cut it out, what's the matter with you?"

"Bobby says that's how you get people to open up."

"Do me a favor. Don't listen to anything else Bobby tells you, okay?"

Bobby's trick didn't work. Even with Charlie yelling "Police," nobody opened their door.

No surprise. Most of the people in the building

work during the day. I hurry down the hallway, go around the bend.

Then I see it.

The last apartment door on the hallway—it's slightly ajar.

"Charlie! Here we go!"

Charlie pounds a few more times on a door, then trots over to see what I'm talking about.

"She must have gone in here," I explain. My chest is still heaving from running up the stairs, and I'm sweating more than ever. I push open the door. Right away I see this gray paint-spattered drop cloth covering the floor like a grimy carpet. And at the same time I smell paint.

Everything in the apartment has been shoved out of the way and covered with sheets of plastic. The walls are shiny white and wet.

Painters.

That rings a bell.

I look at Charlie. I don't know if he's thinking what I'm thinking, but I guess he sees the fear in my face because his face gets all pale, too.

What I'm thinking is—

The apartment is being painted, just like 2-C was painted. Just like last time. It's the—

I feel a gun press into my back.

"Hold it right there," says a gruff voice.

Even though I know I shouldn't, I can't resist turning my head.

And there they are.

Three masked men.

CHAPTER 11

THE MEN WEAR WHITE PAINTER'S MASKS. PAINTERS, I tell myself. Painters. Not robbers. Painters.

"What are you doing in here?" one of the painters barks at me.

I look down at the wooden brush handle that the painter jabbed in my back. Not a gun at all.

"Our c-cat," I stammer out.

"What cat?" asks another painter. "You see any cat?" he asks the other two.

"No cats," says the third painter.

"Here, Fluffy, here, kitty," Charlie calls, wandering off into the apartment.

I'm getting my breath back. "Our cat . . . ran in here, I think," I explain.

"You think?" says the first painter. But his eyes above the white mask don't look so angry anymore.

"Well, you can look," he tells me, "but don't touch anything or take anything, 'cause we'll end up getting blamed, okay?"

"Yeah," agrees the second painter, "last time we were supposed to paint an apartment in this building these robbers came before we got here and . . ."

He waves his paint brush in the air, letting the thought trail off.

Suddenly a bad thought hits me. I say it out loud. "How do I know you're not them? The robbers, I mean."

I can see the surprise in the painters' eyes. Then they start laughing.

"Take a good look around," says the third painter, jabbing his brush at the walls. "You think robbers would waste their time painting like this?"

I look around. He's got a point, I guess. Looks like they're doing a great paint job.

"Denise!" Charlie yells.

"Excuse me."

Following Charlie's voice, I run across three drop cloths, down a hall, and into what looks like a study. Bookcases covered in plastic sheets line all four walls, plus there's a tall ladder propped up next to one of the bookcases. Plus, standing by the window, there's Charlie.

"What is it?" I say. "You find her?"

"No," Charlie says. "That's why I called you."

I stare at him. "What's why you called me?"

"I looked in every room, Denise. She's not here."

Thinking the painters were robbers distracted me

for a second. Distracted me from my real problem. Fluffy.

Now I get a terrible sinking feeling, like I'm sinking all the way back to the first floor. Because if Fluffy's not here, I have no idea where she is.

Dust motes sprinkle down onto my head. A final insult.

Dust motes? Wait a minute. . . .

I look up. And there she is.

Fluffy. Crawling along one of the tall bookcases, her mouth opening and closing in a silent, scared meow.

"Fluffy," I say, "*there* you are!"

But I'm thinking—Oh, great.

Don't get me wrong. I'm relieved that we found her and very happy she's okay. But did she have to go way up there?

Charlie stares up at the cat. "How'd she get up there?"

There's only one answer, and it's staring me right in the face. The ladder.

"I'll get her," Charlie offers.

"Get back."

"Why?"

"Because I'm going to get her," I say, "that's why."

There's no way I'm letting Charlie up this ladder, that's for sure.

"You can't get her," Charlie says.

"Why not? What do you mean I can't get her? Of course I can get her." I put my hands on the ladder.

"Denise," Charlie tells me patiently, like he's talking to a two-year-old, "you're afraid of heights."

"I am not," I lie. "Anyway, I'm afraid of high

heights. You know, cliffs, tops of buildings, that kind of thing. This is just a ladder, Charlie. A stupid ladder. I mean, come on!"

"You get dizzy. Remember at the amusement park?"

"Just move out of the way and hold the ladder," I snap.

Charlie sighs. But he holds the ladder.

But before I can climb up the ladder, he says, "Denise, I could go up there and get her so easy, I'm telling you—"

"Shush."

He shushes. He looks worried, though.

Ridiculous. I start climbing up the rickety ladder.

Up. My least favorite word in the English language.

I climb fast. Trying not to think about it.

I'm about five rungs up when I stop.

This is crazy. But I feel very high up in the air. Like I'm taking an escalator ride into space.

Ooh—and you know what else? I think I am getting a little—

Yes, definitely getting a little dizzy.

I start clutching the sides of the ladder hard. I can feel my sweaty T-shirt clinging to my back, too, like even my shirt is afraid it's going to fall.

Just don't look down, Denise.

Don't look down.

I look down.

Charlie looks so far away.

And then the whole room starts to spin very slowly, this way, then back.

"Denise?" Charlie calls, looking very worried. "Are you okay?"

"Yeah."

I look away from Charlie. But the room keeps spinning, faster and faster. I look up. "Come here, Fluffy, that's a good girl," I call.

Fluffy doesn't move.

From outside on the street I hear the crowd gasp. Like maybe they're looking in the window and they can't believe I'm so high up the ladder.

Right.

If the crowd is gasping it means that guy on the roof is doing something crazy, like dancing along the edge of Hamilton House.

In one way, it's been good having Fluffy and the robbers to worry about—it helped me forget about that guy on the roof.

Well, this is not the time I wanted to be reminded about that guy, let me tell you. 'Cause the whole room is starting to fade to black. Like someone is slowly dimming the lights.

I think I'm going to puke.

Better hurry.

Get Fluffy, Denise.

Get Fluffy!

Somehow I manage to unlock my left hand from the rail of the ladder. I hold my hand out toward Fluffy. She shrinks back.

"Denise, come back down," Charlie pleads.

"Jump! Jump!"

It's faint. The voices. At first I think they're all in my head. Like I'm really losing my mind. Then I

realize where they're coming from. Outside. Down
the street. The crowd is yelling for him to—
   "Jump! Jump!"
   I reach out wildly for Fluffy. But she shrinks back
farther, hissing, and swipes at me and—
   I duck back but—
   Now I'm rocking back and forth—
   Losing my balance and—
   "DENISE!" yells Charlie.
   As . . . I . . . fall!

CHAPTER 12

CRASH!

The ladder falls.

I grab onto the bookcase, kicking books out with my feet.

I'm okay! I didn't fall.

Only I don't know how much longer I can hold on to this bookcase and—

What if the whole bookcase topples over? It could land on—

"Charlie! Get out of the room! Now!"

I turn my head slightly. I can see Charlie. He's trying to set the ladder back up. But he can't. It's too big and he's too little. And the bookcase is starting to wobble back and forth and back and—

"CHARLIE! GET OUT OF HERE RIGHT NOW!"

There's a thunder of footsteps as—

In rush the painters. "Hang on!" someone yells at me. I hang on. The painters set up the ladder. Someone just about runs up the ladder, it sounds like. I guess the painters aren't scared of heights.

I feel two strong hands around my middle and another pair of hands placing my sneakers back on the rungs of the ladder.

My legs don't move. I feel paralyzed.

I think one of the painters carried me down to the floor.

Yes, that must be what happened, because now I'm sitting on the floor. I watch as one of the painters scrambles up the ladder and gets Fluffy down. He hands the frightened cat to Charlie.

Then one of the other painters helps me up. "You okay?"

"Yeah," I manage to say.

And before I know it Charlie and I are back in the hallway with Fluffy purring in Charlie's arms and not a scratch on any one of us.

"Take that cat back to your apartment," one of the painters advises us.

"Oh, we will," I promise.

The painter closes the door. I hear him lock it, too. I stare straight ahead as Charlie, Fluffy and I wait for the elevator.

Everything is fine, I tell myself.

This is true, but it's like it's taking my body a while to get the message. My body still seems to feel like it's up on top of the ladder.

"That's so great," Charlie tells me, petting Fluffy.

I'm pushing the down button that calls the

elevator. I'm pushing it over and over. Now here's a word I like. *Down.*

"What's great?" I ask hollowly.

"The way you got over your fear of heights."

"What are you talking about?"

"You went up the ladder."

"Yeah, *right.*"

"You did."

"Charlie, I fell off the ladder."

"Yeah, but first you went up. That means you're cured."

I try to grin at him. "I came very close to ralphing my guts out on your head, Charlie. I'm not cured at all. A stupid stinking ladder. I didn't even know I had it this bad. I'm serious, Charlie. I think I need to see a shrink."

He shrugs. "Why? You're all better."

At last the elevator doors open.

And there's Bobby, eating a tuna-fish-on-a-bagel sandwich. He's got tuna smeared all around his mouth and he's dropping little bits of tuna onto the elevator floor with each bite.

"Hey." He waves a bottle of chocolate soda at us with his other hand. "You found the cat. Excellent. See, I told you there wouldn't be any problem."

Fluffy starts squirming in Charlie's arms and meowing.

"You got her?" I ask my brother.

"Uh-huh."

"Here, let me take her."

Charlie turns fast, pulling Fluffy away from me. "I got her!"

I glare at Bobby. "This was all your fault, Bobby. All of it."

Bobby laughs. Let him laugh. The way he's going, eating everything in sight, he'll be the first twelve-year-old in history to drop dead of a heart attack.

"You guys want to come for a ride?" he asks. "Or you want to wait and catch the elevator on the way down?"

At the moment the thought of going up, up, up is extremely unpleasant to me.

"We'll wait," I tell him.

"Suit yourself. Oh, hey, Chuck—I got you some gum."

He tosses out a pack of cinnamon gum, which lands on the floor in front of Charlie. Then he presses "Door Close." The big metal doors start to shut.

"Careful," I tell Charlie, who is reaching for the gum.

Which is when Fluffy gets away from Charlie. She springs through the closing doors onto the elevator and starts gulping down the tuna fish that Bobby dropped on the floor.

I step forward, but it's too late. The big metal doors are almost all the way shut.

"Bobby!" I yell.

As Charlie reaches out his hand.

The large metal doors close right on his tiny fingers.

CHAPTER 13

THE DOORS OPEN AGAIN RIGHT AWAY.

I pull Charlie back, flop down on the floor, and gently take his arm. He looks shocked. His hand hangs down limply. "Let me see!" I cry. "Charlie! Let me see!"

He lets me look at the hand. I just stare at it. How do you tell if a hand is broken?

"You okay?" I ask him. "Does it hurt?"

Charlie looks at his hand in amazement. In one second he's going to burst into tears and I'm going to have to go call 911. Here we go.

Instead, Charlie giggles.

"Wow," he says. "I didn't get hurt at all." He looks up. "Thanks, Bobby. You saved my life."

I turn.

On the elevator, Bobby has his finger on the

"Door Open" button. Fluffy licks a spot of tuna fish on the floor, over and over.

"You see how I stopped this baby just in the nick of time?" Bobby tells me. He whistles. "What reflexes. Whew! Well, Denise, you owe me one."

"Thanks," I say, "for giving me ten nightmares. You're a walking disaster area, Bobby Lawrence."

"Fine, be that way," Bobby says, grinning. "Adios, amigos." He presses a button—

"No!" I yell.

But the doors slide shut.

And the elevator rises.

"So long, suckers!" I hear Bobby shout.

And then his cackle.

And then . . . nothing.

CHAPTER 14

So it's back to the dark, smelly, roach-infested stairs for me and Charlie as we try to jog up from the sixth floor to the thirteenth floor, where Bobby lives.

You know what? I forgot how much running we've been doing. We had trouble running up the stairs the first time. And by now Charlie and I are both totally pooped.

Yeah, I guess it would have been faster to wait for the elevator. 'Cause we have to take a long rest break on the landing of the tenth floor, hanging on the banister, both of us gasping for air.

"Hey, Denise," says Charlie.

"Yeah."

"Look at that."

"What?"

"Look down."

I look down. Then I remember. What I'm always telling myself. Don't look down.

Too late. Because I'm already looking down at the inside of the stairwell, where you can see the banisters zigzagging themselves all the way down to the basement. Eleven flights. It's like a picture of how it feels when you fall.

"Sorry," Charlie tells me, patting my back as I close my eyes and take deep breaths. "I forgot."

"That's okay."

"You look green," he tells me.

I try to smile. "I am green. Here, let me tie those laces. Stop it! Hold still."

He lets me tie them. Then we trudge up the last two flights of stairs. Ring Bobby's bell.

And guess what?

He won't come to the door.

Silently calling him every name I can think of, I keep my finger on the buzzer, pressing hard. Charlie keeps pounding and kicking the door, too.

No answer.

"Maybe he went down to look for us," Charlie suggests.

"No," I tell him, "he's just trying to get me mad."

Behind us, the elevator doors glide open. Charlie and I turn.

But it's not Bobby, it's Mrs. Carmen, shuffling off the elevator, using her cane. I hurry over to the elevator and hold the doors open for her.

"Oh, thanks, Denise," she says. "You're a great help." She's got her rent envelope in her hand, which the co-op board sticks in your mailbox once a month. "How am I going to pay this?" she mutters, shaking her head. "I haven't even paid last month's yet."

Mrs. Carmen fumbles for her keys. She lives right next door to Bobby in 13-E. I feel sorry for her, having to worry about money so much. But my family is the same way.

On the other hand, here's a reason I should feel really sorry for her. She's got Bobby as a neighbor.

Mrs. Carmen opens the door to her apartment as Charlie goes back to slapping Bobby's door.

"If you're looking for Bobby he's downstairs in the lobby," she adds before she shuts her door.

The lobby?

Could Charlie be right? Did Bobby go down to look for us?

I hear Mrs. Carmen lock her door—three times. I stare at the closed door for a second, like even that closed door puzzles me. Then I turn back to the elevator.

The elevator must have gone down while we were talking to Mrs. Carmen. Because right now the arrow points to floor three. And it's rising.

4 . . . 5 . . . 6 . . .

Charlie and I wait, watching the elevator like cats sitting outside a mouse hole.

The doors open.

There stands Bobby with a rolled up *Newsweek* in his pudgy hand. And no cat.

"Hey," Bobby says in that high voice of his as he takes out his keys.

He starts unlocking his door. He's got this calm,

serious air about him, like nothing special is going on. It drives me crazy.

"WHERE'S FLUFFY?!" I shout.

"Ow!" Bobby says, giving me an angry look. "That was right in my ear. What's the matter with you?"

"What's the matter with *me*?"

He opens the door. "Fluffy's in my apartment. Where do you thinks she is?" He holds up the magazine. "Just went down to get our mail. Ya mind?"

Yes, I mind. I mind very much. But right now I just want to get Fluffy and go back downstairs. And I feel like if I open my mouth to tell Bobby what I think of him, I won't ever be able to shut it again. So I chew on my bead necklace and don't say a word.

Bobby's apartment is one of the fancy ones, as you can imagine it would be with movie producers for parents. All the furniture is new and black and shiny and looks like it's made out of glass. The chairs have these sharp angles that could kill you if you sit down too quick.

Bobby picks up a remote and flicks on this gigundo TV screen. "Hey, Chuck, you want to watch cartoons in 3-D? I have special glasses."

"For real?"

I storm into the living room, looking all around for Fluffy. "Well? Where is she?" I say.

Bobby looks at me, surprised. "How should I know?"

"Well, you better find her," I tell him. "Or else."

"Or else what?"

You know something? You should always have an

answer in mind when you say "or else." Because I didn't have an answer in mind, and now it feels like it's way too late for me to think of one. So I just stand here.

Charlie says, "Or else we'll have to find her ourselves."

He thinks he's helping me out, but Bobby bursts out laughing. Charlie laughs, too. He's pleased that he made Bobby laugh, though I can tell he's not sure what the joke is.

Blushing with fury and embarrassment, I rush off down the hall calling "Fluffy! Fluffy!"

"Don't go in my room," Bobby advises me, lumbering down the hall behind me. "The maid was off this week and it's starting to smell really foul in there."

"Thanks for the warning." I stick my head into the bathroom. There are dirty clothes hanging over the shower pole. There's an odd dusty rectangle on the floor. But there's no Fluffy.

"I opened the window really wide," Bobby goes on, "but I can't seem to get the smell out. I think maybe I left some food lying around and it's rotting or something."

I stop short. "You did what?"

"He left the window open," Charlie answers for him.

I start running. The door to his room is ajar. I fling it open. "Fluffy?!"

Bobby was telling the truth. The room does smell bad. Like he's got rotten eggs in his underwear drawer. I don't see the cat. But I do see a wide-open window, the curtains gently blowing in the spring breeze. Shouts from the mob scene down the block float up to me. *Jump! Jump!*

"Fluffy?" I call, more quietly now. My voice shakes a little.

'Cause if there's one rule Ms. Orson has gone over with me about a hundred times, it's that I should never open one of her windows. 'Cause Fluffy could jump out.

She's worried about Fluffy jumping out on the first floor.

This is the thirteenth.

If Fluffy jumped out up here—

"Uh-oh," says Charlie as he walks slowly toward the window.

"What's the matter?" Bobby asks.

"Charlie," I cry, "get away from that window!"

"I'm just going to look."

"NO!"

"Here," Charlie says to me, "I'll go down on my knees. See? This is totally safe, Denise. See?"

He's kneeling down. I guess he's right. That is safe. He sticks his head out the window. He keeps it out there a long time. I don't say a word.

"What?" asks Bobby. "Hey, you don't think the cat would—?"

I guess he gets his answer from my face.

"Oh no," he says.

"Charlie?" I ask. Barely any sound comes out.

Charlie pulls his head back inside the apartment. He's crying.

I rush to the window. But I only get about halfway there. Then I have to go along the wall, creeping my way over. Bobby's already looking out the window by the time I get there. I try to look, too. It's a struggle. I have to clutch the sides of the window frame for a while before I can stick my head outside, and then I have to keep my eyes closed for a few more seconds before I can look down.

Wow.

We're up high.

It's like my eyes fly out of my head and zoom all the way down until they splat like eggs on the sidewalk below. I can see that big crowd of people down the block, all waiting for the man to jump. Only now the spectators all look as tiny as Mr. Slocum did when I looked up at him from the street.

It's a struggle just keeping my eyes open. But I keep looking down.

I can see our red awning . . . and that big moving truck . . . and the three moving men . . . and the little green dot of the cap on Fernando's head . . .

And then—

Oh no.

Right under this window. Thirteen stories down. Lies poor little Fluffy.

She's stretched out on the sidewalk like a little white bath mat.

Smeared with blood.

I BACK INTO THE ROOM, GASPING FOR AIR. CHARLIE'S crying, saying, "Fluffy, Fluffy!" And Bobby's—

Laughing?

You know . . . Bobby may be a rotten kid, but I can't believe he'd be laughing if . . .

I force myself to look out the window again.

There's the little white body that looks so much like a white bath mat. . . .

And suddenly I'm remembering that dusty rectangle on the floor in Bobby's bathroom. The rectangle where the white bath mat used to be.

"Bob-by," I say slowly. "You little—"

Bobby falls onto his bed, rocking back and forth as he guffaws. "You should have seen the look on your face!"

He tries to lift his stubby legs in the air. "That's

my mom's bath mat," he finally manages to gasp out. "I smeared some ketchup on it and put it down there while I was waiting for you guys to come upstairs. I told Fernando not to let anyone move it. Perfect! Perfect! I'm a genius!" He claps with glee.

"Where's Fluffy?" I ask, my heart pounding.

Bobby gets off the bed and walks over to the sliding doors of his closet. He slides open the doors. "Ta-da!"

I stare at the cluttered closet, with all the old video games and other expensive junk Bobby owns.

Oh, please, I pray. Please let that cat be all—

A little white face appears, staring up at me with frightened gray eyes.

Fluffy!

I kneel down next to her. So does Charlie. "Oh, sweet little baby," I say. "You good little girl."

"You little goo-goo," gurgles Charlie, stroking her back.

I want to throw my arms around Fluffy and hug her hard, but you can't do that with cats. So I force myself to just hold out my hand. Fluffy stares at my hand for a second, then bumps her jaw against it, rubbing me over and over.

"You're good," I whisper into the cat's ear. I kiss the top of her head. Then I raise my voice. "I don't know what kind of sick person locks a cat in a closet, but I gotta tell you, Bobby, I'm very worried about you."

Bobby grins down at me. "Good joke, huh?"

"I am, Bobby. I'm worried. They say that's how serial killers get started, by torturing little animals."

"She looks okay," Bobby observes. As if to prove Bobby's point, Fluffy flops on her back on the rug and rolls around happily. And when Bobby sits down with us and starts to pet her, she purrs. The little traitor.

Flap flap flap flap . . .

Sounds like an umbrella opening and closing.

I stand up fast.

Sure enough, a pigeon just landed on Bobby's windowsill.

"Hey," says Charlie, excited.

"Bobby?" I say, my heart pounding.

The pigeon coos as it struts up and down the sill, staring into the bedroom with a tiny pink eye. Its head bobs up and down.

"Uh-oh," says Bobby.

Bobby looks down at Fluffy. Fluffy crouches down. Her little white tail slowly swishes back and forth. Her gray eyes point straight at the open window—and the bird.

"FLUFFY!" I cry. "NO!"

Fluffy races across the carpet toward the pigeon on the ledge.

The pigeon squawks as it flies away.

Fluffy jumps out the window.

CHAPTER 16

A FEW PIGEON FEATHERS FLOAT DOWN INTO THE room.

Then there's silence.

I stare at the wide-open window, too horrified to breathe.

I gotta tell you. This is the most disgusting sight I ever saw. The way that sweet little cat went right out the window. Poof! Just like that.

Gone.

"Oh, wow," Charlie says. "Oh, wow."

His face twists. He's crying again. So is Bobby, tears silently streaming down his big cheeks like they did that day at the playground when the bully kept calling him Blobby.

Hey? You know what I just realized? I'm crying, too.

Then I hear this little meow.

We all race to the window.

Like a lot of tall apartment houses, the Westholme has this little six-inch ledge that runs around the whole outside of the building under the windows on the thirteenth floor. For decoration, I guess. That's what I'm looking at right now, that ledge.

Down on that ledge, looking up at me, sits Fluffy.

She made it onto the ledge! She didn't fall! She's alive! Charlie and Bobby and I are all screaming.

"Oh, Fluffy!" I gush. "Fluffy! Fluffy!"

Even though it's warm, Fluffy shivers. She's several feet away from me. It's not like I can reach her and pull her back inside. But I feel so thrilled— it's like I was dead for five minutes and now I came back to life.

And now that I know Fluffy is still alive, and I can think straight again, I realize something else. I realize that I'm leaning out an open window on the thirteenth—

Ow!

Oops.

I just ducked back inside the window so fast I banged my head on the window frame and then crashed hard into Bobby and Charlie.

"What's wrong?" Bobby asks me, looking worried again. "Come on, we gotta get her! We gotta get Fluffy!"

"I know, I know," I say, holding up my hand like a traffic cop. "Give me a sec, okay?"

I'm breathing in and out hard, like Elise Miller,

this girl in my class at Parker School who always gets asthma attacks during gym.

"She's scared of heights," Charlie explains.

"Then let me get the cat," offers Bobby.

This is one of the few times in my life that I've ever respected Bobby. But the way I see it, Fluffy is my responsibility. Even it if is all Bobby's fault that she got out of Ms. Orson's apartment in the first place. And also all Bobby's fault that she's out on the ledge on the thirteenth floor.

"Thanks," I say, "for offering. I mean it."

Bobby beams.

I'd love to let Bobby get Fluffy. But here's the deal. I don't want to trust Fluffy's life to anyone else. Certainly not Bobby of all people. And I'm sure not letting Charlie lean out this window and dangle over the street. That only leaves—

"No," I say, sawing the air with my hands. "I'm going to do it. But Bobby, you can help."

"I can?"

"Yeah. You have to hold my legs. I'm going to lean out there and get her."

"No!" yells Charlie, stamping his foot. He rushes at me and tries to pull me back from the window. "That's a bad idea, Denise. You can't do it! You—"

"I'm going to lean out and get her," I repeat. I feel like I'm trying to convince myself as much as Charlie.

"You!" I point at Charlie. Then I point to the other side of Bobby's room. "Over there."

As Charlie backs away, Bobby crouches down and holds my legs. He's got his big head down. I feel like he's begging my forgiveness. That feels good.

I wait until I feel him get a good grip on my blue jeans. "Hey," I say to Charlie, who's creeping back across the carpet toward me like we're playing Red Light, Green Light. "Get back. More. More. Now stay there."

Oh, please, hold on tight, Bobby, I pray. I would like to live to be fourteen.

"You got me?" I ask Bobby.

"I got you."

"Don't let go!"

He doesn't bother to answer. I guess it's a stupid instruction. Like he's really going to forget to hold on. I guess I'm just stalling.

Then . . .

I lean out the window, spreading my arms wide like I'm doing a slow-motion swan dive.

There's the crowd down the street, all waiting for the man to jump off the roof. Hey, folks. We got some more drama over here in this window, if you'd just turn your heads a sec.

But they've all got their eyes glued on the roof of Hamilton House. If I fall out of this window to my death, they probably won't even notice.

I lean farther out.

Far enough to realize that Charlie is right. This is a very very very bad idea. I'm going to faint. Or at least I'm going to throw up, either onto that bright red awning or all over Fernando.

I'm leaning so far out that my head points down, like I'm falling. Down to where the big moving truck now looks about two inches long.

I'm not falling, mind you, I'm just hanging here.

But with my head down this way, my body keeps telling me that I'm falling, and that's bad enough.

Whoops.

My Yankees cap, which I wear absolutely everywhere, just flew off my head.

Well, I sure can't worry about that now.

So much blood is rushing into my face that my eyes squinch up, making it a little hard for me to see.

"Okay, Fluffy," I say, slowly reaching toward her.

Fluffy's not looking at me. She's all hunkered down. Then my fingertips brush her back.

Her head jerks up. She's so startled to see me that—

She starts to slip right off the ledge.

CHAPTER 17

I GRAB FOR FLUFFY. BUT I CAN'T REACH HER.

Her claws scribble-scrabble against the ledge as she slips and slides.

I'm screaming.

But Fluffy makes it back on the ledge somehow. Wow.

If it's true what they say, that cats have nine lives, I figure little Fluffy is down to around three.

"Okay, Fluffy," I say, slowly reaching for her again. "Don't get scared. It's just me."

I can see her head, upside down, watching me as I move my hands slowly closer—

Closer . . .

"DENISE! I CAN'T HOLD YOU!" Bobby suddenly screams.

I feel my legs lifting up into the air and—

My whole body slides out and down!

CHAPTER 18

I SCREAM AND—

Grab the stone wall of the building, clutching so hard I chip my nails and scratch my fingers but—

Wait a minute. WAIT A MINUTE! I'm not falling.

No. Bobby still has ahold of my legs.

"UP!" I scream. "UP! UP!"

I wrestle and wriggle my way back into the room.

Even when I'm standing inside the apartment, my heart pounds like a Super Ball bouncing around my chest.

And Bobby—

This is really too much.

Bobby is laughing.

He stops laughing when he sees the look on my face, though. I'll give him that.

"I had you the whole time," he says. "I was just—"

I raise my hands in fists. "YOU COULD HAVE KILLED ME!" I scream.

Bobby's mouth drops open. He looks hurt. "No way," he insists. "Oh, come on, Denise. You don't think—It was a lousy thing to do, okay, I admit it, but it wasn't dangerous. Really. Not even a little teensy—oomph—"

Charlie charges into Bobby's knees, and even though Bobby is about a hundred times Charlie's size, the surprise works for Charlie. Bobby goes down in a heap.

Unbelievable. I let Bobby tease me. It takes Charlie to knock him down.

Charlie's punching Bobby in the belly, which can't hurt Bobby too much. But I pull Charlie off him.

"It's okay," I yell at Charlie, holding his little arms, which are windmilling as he tries to throw more punches. "I'm okay. It's okay. Charlie! Stop!"

"You big stupid!" Charlie yells at Bobby. "You could have killed my sister!"

Bobby sits up. Tears form in the corners of his big dark eyes. Can you believe it? Charlie's only six, and Bobby is afraid of him. "Guys, please. I was just goofing," he says, looking away.

Just what Charlie said to me when he played Man on the Roof. So that's where Charlie picked up that expression. Of course.

"Look . . . I'm sorry," Bobby says, crying harder. "Why are you guys . . . being so mean? I was just—just trying to be funny."

Unbelievable. Bobby nearly drops me out a twelve-story window, and I feel sorry for *him*.

"Bobby?" I ask finally.

"Yeah?"

"Do you realize that we're in the middle of an emergency here? Do you realize that Ms. Orson's cat is out on the ledge?"

"Yeah." He snuffles.

"So do you think this is a good time for goofing?"

"I'm sorry, Denise. I said I was sorry. I mean it." He wipes his nose with his hand. "You know how I like to kid around."

I sigh. Then sigh again. Then sigh a third time. "Okay, I'm sorry, too," I say finally. "And . . . now let's get to work, okay?"

Bobby grins at me hopefully. Charlie smiles from ear to ear. It's like now we're a team or something. We all look out the window.

Fluffy's gone.

My stomach does a three-sixty.

Then I see her.

She's chasing another pigeon down the ledge. She's way out of reach. Bobby's bedroom window is the last window in his apartment. The next window is Mrs. Carmen's. Fluffy's right smack in between.

"Super," I say, stalking out of Bobby's bedroom.

"What's super about it?" Bobby calls after me.

"No," I explain, "I'm calling the super. You got the number?"

Bobby yells out that I should look on the fridge. Sure enough, I find the building superintendent's number at the bottom of a typed list of emergency numbers held on the fridge with an ice-cream-cone magnet. I call. No answer. I leave a message.

Terrific. Now what?

Then I take another look at that list of emergency numbers. Hey, this is sure an emergency. . . .

From the moment I dial, I start feeling calmer.

Now this will all be out of my hands.

And soon it will all be over. And everything will be—

"Fire department, is this an emergency?"

"It sure is. This is Denise Alexander at 365 West End Avenue. I'd like to report a cat on the ledge outside of Apartment 13-D as in Dumb."

"A what?"

"A cat on the ledge."

There's a sigh. "Where are you?"

I repeat the address.

"What is that?" the man asks. "Seventy-eighth Street?"

"That's right."

"Kid, have you looked out your window? We've got a man on the roof over there. We've got everybody and everybody's uncle right on your block trying to get the guy to come down."

"Terrific," I say, "so please have some of those people and those uncles come over to my building to help with the cat."

Another sigh. "I'll be honest with you, kid. We don't do cats anymore. I mean, even if we had the time and the manpower, which we do not, we don't do cats. Insurance. You know."

I can feel the back of my neck starting to itch. "Insurance?"

"Cats go out windows, kid. Fact of life. But if we try to save them, it raises our insurance rates through the roof, 'cause pet owners could sue us if the cat dies. You see?"

I don't really see. Instead I'm thinking about what Ms. Orson could do to me if Fluffy—

She wouldn't sue me, of course. She'd just feel so sad and horrible that I would not want to live.

The man at the fire department apologizes, then says he has to go. The line goes dead.

Looks like—

I'm on my own.

In a way, it's not a bad feeling.

"I can handle this," I tell myself.

Whatever it takes.

Then Bobby screams.

CHAPTER 19

I RUN BACK INTO THE BEDROOM. BOBBY'S GOT his hands over his face. He's blubbering. "It's not my fault!" he yells when he sees me. "I tried to stop him! Denise, you've got to—"

"Where's Charlie?!" I shout at him.

"I told him not to, I begged him, I tried to grab him, but—"

"WHERE'S CHARLIE?!"

Bobby points at the window.

My first thought is that Bobby is fooling me again. That Charlie's hiding under the bed or something. But Bobby would have to be the world's greatest actor to be crying the way he is and faking it.

I run to the window.

"I told him not to go out there," sobs Bobby. "I begged him."

Well, at least Charlie's not dead—yet.

That's the good news.

I can see him.

Now here's the very very very bad news.

Charlie's out on the ledge.

For real.

CHAPTER 20

I STICK MY HEAD OUT THE WINDOW. "CHARLIE," I SAY, not wanting to talk loud and scare him but wanting to make sure he hears me. "Charlie, don't move. You get me? You have to stay where you are."

Charlie has his back pressed up hard against the wall of the building, his sneakers splayed out so they fit on the narrow ledge. His shoelaces, I notice, have come untied.

"Denise?" he asks.

My throat's so dry I can barely answer him. "Yeah?"

"I'm sorry." His voice is tiny, scared.

"Why are you sorry?"

"I shouldn't have come out here. I just wanted to get Fluffy. I—I knew you wanted Fluffy."

I don't know if I'm sweating or crying or what.

But I can feel this wetness running in and out of my eyes. I have to keep blinking. It's like the whole world has disappeared. And all I see is Charlie, floating in space.

"That's right," I answer him. "You wanted to help me. And that's great, Charlie. It's great, it's great."

If I ever get my brother back inside, I figure Mom and Dad will scream at him for about a year and teach him a lesson about going out on ledges. But that's for later.

"Now," I say, "all you have to do is stay right where you are and we're going to get you down. Okay? There's fire trucks down there. No, Charlie— DON'T LOOK DOWN! Just listen to me. That's right. There are fire trucks down there. They're here to get that guy off the roof. Remember? Well, I'm going to send Bobby down and he's going to tell them to come over here and get *you* down. You understand?"

"I'm going to fall."

"You're not going to fall, Charlie. Listen to me! You are not going to fall!"

Charlie is silent. His eyes are closed. Finally he answers me. Only what he says breaks my heart. "For real?"

"For real, Charlie!" I yell at him. "For real!"

I have to wait for a wave of tears to pass before I can say, "Okay, stay right there and don't look down or anything and—"

"Maybe I can make it back."

"NO! Don't try. Just—Charlie! What are you . . . ? Charlie! Listen to me!"

But Charlie isn't listening. He's inching his way
back along the tiny ledge toward me. Only—
He starts to teeter and—
His little body jerks back and forth and—
His arms flail and he—

CHAPTER 21

HE DIDN'T FALL. HE DIDN'T FALL. DENISE, he didn't fall because there he is. There's my brother. He's still on the ledge. Somehow—don't ask me how—he regained his balance.

Thank you. Thank you thank you thank you thank you.

I lean way out the window so Charlie can hear me loud and clear. "Charlie Alexander, you move again I'm going to kill you, you understand? I mean it. I'm coming out to get you. Stay right there. I gotta get something. I'll be like one minute here. Then I'm coming."

Back in the room, I see this big heavy kid. He stares at me, his round face pale and wet with tears. I stare back at Bobby in amazement. I almost don't recognize him. I forgot he was here.

"It's okay," I stammer as I rush to the bed, "it's going to be okay. Help me strip your bed."

Without a word, he starts helping me rip the sheets off his messy bed. Moving as fast as I've ever moved in my life, I tie the top sheet to the bottom sheet with a big knot. Then I hand one end to Bobby. "Pull," I order.

We have a brief tug-of-war, making the knot between the two sheets ultratight.

"What are you doing?" Bobby whispers.

No time to explain. I rush past him, trailing the two sheets like a tail. I tie one end of the sheet around the leg of the radiator, yanking with all my might to make the knot tight, tight, tight. Then I tie the other end around my stomach. I lean back, letting the sheets hold my weight, like I'm water-skiing and the radiator is the motorboat.

The rope holds.

I sling one leg over the windowsill.

If you told me this morning that I'd be climbing out a thirteenth-story window, I would have bet you a million dollars you were wrong.

Well, I lose, I tell myself.

Then I close my eyes.

I have to take one last deep breath.

I can't believe I'm doing this. But I don't have time to believe it or not believe it because—

Good-bye, fear of heights!

I'm going out the window.

CHAPTER 22

WEST END AVENUE IS A CANYON OF TALL BUILDINGS. The wind whistles right through. It feels like the icy air is trying to blast me right off the ledge.

Oh wow. Oh wow.

"Charlie, it's okay, here I come."

I'm not coming fast, believe me. I'm inching little tiny parts of an inch at a time.

I'm staring straight ahead, which means I'm staring across the street. Big apartment buildings are like huge stacks of TV sets, each window showing a different channel. I see all sorts of people inside the hundreds of apartments in the tall buildings across the way. For some reason I focus on a bored maid in a pink dress. She slowly pushes a vacuum cleaner around a room.

Just don't look down, I tell myself. Whatever you do, Denise, do not not not not not look down.

I look down.

I moan.

It's like the street sucks me down, like a vacuum cleaner. Like the street wants me to fall. Like the street wants to smack me to death with one giant SMACK!

Okay, so I'm not over my fear of heights. My fear of heights is right here with me. I'm just going to have to live with it, that's all. Otherwise Charlie and I are going to die.

Charlie's shaking all over.

"It's okay," I tell him. "I'm coming."

Telling myself, It's okay, Denise, you can do this. You can do this.

I slide farther out along the ledge.

When I was inside, it didn't look like Charlie went so far along this ledge. Now that I'm out here, it's a different story. An inch of ledge goes a long way when you're up thirteen stories. Charlie went a long way before he got scared. A very long way.

I slide out farther. The sheet trails behind me. Half of the first sheet now stretches out the window. Two thirds. Then the whole first sheet goes out the window. I know, because I can see the big fat knot.

I take another step.

Then suddenly my right hand, the one that's leading the way along the wall, feels—

What?

I turn my head slightly to see what I'm holding. Black wires.

I know what these are. TV wires. Cable. Huh. I guess Mrs. Carmen gets cable. I never would have thought she could afford it.

I'm losing my mind. Fear has driven me bonkers. What difference does it make what these black wires are for? That's really what I should be worrying about at this moment—the wires.

"Denise?" calls Charlie, his voice cracking.

"Here I come," I tell him. I shuffle my feet, moving farther along the ledge.

Wow. Look who's here. More pigeons. Sitting on the ledge like little old men on a park bench. I keep nudging them with my feet as I inch along the ledge. They fly up a little to get out of my way, then settle back down.

Then it hits me. For the first time since that pigeon first flew onto Bobby's ledge, it hits me. There are pigeons on the thirteenth floor! So high up! You know, maybe Bobby is right. Maybe there are pigeons on the moon. Ha-ha-ha-ha-ha-ha-ha-ha-ha-ha—

Denise, get a grip!

Okay—okay—I'm almost there. Come on, Denise. Come on.

I reach for Charlie's hand. He clutches my hand, my clothes. I've got him! Bobby cheers from the window as something—

It's a pigeon! Flying right at my head!

Charlie and I both duck and—

I feel my shoes slipping off the ledge, and—

I'm pulling Charlie with me as we both—

F
A
L
L
L
L
L
L
L
L
L
L
L
L
L
L
L
L
L
L
L
L
L
L
L
L
L

CHAPTER 23

WHAM!

My whole body jerks violently and—

Did I just splat against the pavement?

Am I dead?

No, I'm swinging and hugging Charlie and Charlie's hugging me and—

Now I get it. We're hanging by the sheet that's tied around my middle. And that means—

WE'RE DANGLING THIRTEEN STORIES OVER WEST END AVENUE!

And for the first time since I fell I become aware that I'm screaming. And Charlie is screaming. And our screams mix together to make one giant scream, which is lost in the middle of all the sirens and screams from Hamilton House, down the block.

I grab the sheet with my free hand, yelling at Charlie to grab on as well.

So now we're both holding the sheet and holding each other as we swing back and forth, back and forth.

"HOLD ON!" Bobby screams down at us from the window.

Great advice.

"I'LL GET HELP!"

Great idea.

Then I feel the rope starting to pull us up. Bobby's pulling up the rope! Go, Bobby, go!

We only rise an inch, then fall back down again.

"I CAN'T PULL YOU UP!" Bobby screams. "I'M NOT STRONG ENOUGH! CAN YOU HANG ON? I'LL GO GET HELP!"

No, we can't hang on. Not for long. Why doesn't he go get help? He says he's going to go get help but he doesn't, he just—

"GO GET HELP!" I shout at him.

But Bobby just keeps staring down at us, terrified and helpless and paralyzed.

We're going to die! We're going to die unless—

"Charlie!" I'm yelling, even though my head is pressed right up ahead his. "We have to climb up the rope. Can you climb up the rope?"

"Yeah!"

"Good boy!"

We both climb up the rope together, our fists and our bodies all tangled so that I can't even tell which is which and who's who.

Maybe we can climb back to the window.

Who am I kidding? I never climbed even halfway up that big hairy rope in gym.

But this is different. This is life or—

Charlie and I keep climbing. Hand over fist. Hand over fist. Except my arms have now turned into strands of limp spaghetti. I don't think I can go much farther. I don't even think I can hold on to the rope, even if it means dying.

Charlie's face is beet red from the strain. I don't think he can last much longer either.

"DENISE!"

Bobby's scream is piercing. I look up.

And right away I see what he's so upset about.

Above our heads—

The knot in between the two sheets . . . ?

It's starting to come undone.

CHAPTER 24

I STARE UP AT BOBBY. HE STARES DOWN AT ME.

I open my mouth.

No words come out.

Suddenly the knot comes halfway undone with a SNAP!

Charlie and I drop several inches.

Then the knot lets go.

CHAPTER 25

YOU KNOW WHAT?

The only thing that just came between me and Charlie and death is Mrs. Carmen's cable-TV subscription. 'Cause as the knot in the sheet came undone, Charlie and I grabbed onto those black TV wires. And then we both climbed back to the ledge.

That's where we are now.

The ledge.

I never thought that standing on this narrow ledge would feel safe, but it does.

I'm coughing. My lungs hurt. My arms kill. I feel light as a feather. And I've never been this happy.

We made it back to the ledge!

Bobby cheers and claps from the window. I look at Charlie. He looks at me. We're both too worn-out and too scared to smile, but it's like we're smiling at each other without moving our mouths.

Then I see Fluffy.

She must have chased that pigeon farther down the ledge. 'Cause now she's over by the fire escape.

The pigeon is gone. But there's old Fluffy—going up the fire-escape steps. Up to the fourteenth floor.

And we're here on the thirteenth-floor ledge—closer to Mrs. Carmen's window than to Bobby's window. So first I untie the useless sheet from my middle so we don't trip over it. Then I tell Charlie, "This way," and we start inching toward the window. "And watch your laces," I tell him.

We slide-slide-slide our way over to Mrs. Carmen's window. The window's open. I can see Mrs. Carmen's shabby apartment, all this rotten ripped furniture plus a huge new Aiwa CD sound system. And there's Mrs. Carmen on the phone.

"Yeah," she says, "I want the extra-large-screen TV. I'll pay cash on delivery. That's right. And I want—"

Then her jaw drops and the phone drops from her hand as—

Charlie and I drop into her apartment.

She screams.

I hold up my hands. "Mrs. Carmen. We're okay. We're idiots. But we're okay. We won't ever go out the window again. Believe me. See, uh, our cat's safe now. She went up the fourteenth floor. Well. See ya."

Mrs. Carmen is still screaming.

Charlie and I both run.

Except Charlie trips on his laces and goes down.

And now I'm giggling out of control. I'm so glad to be inside. And it's so funny to me that *now* Charlie trips.

Bobby meets us in the hall, hugging both of us in one of those death grips of his. We're all laughing. It feels great.

This time we catch the elevator. It's like everything's going our way now, like magic. We ride up to floor fourteen. We pound on the door of Penthouse C. The door swings open.

The huge apartment is totally empty. There's Mrs. Potter, this rich old lady who always wears lots of jewelry. She's talking to the three movers, signing some forms. Looks like the move is done.

"Hi, Mrs. Potter," Bobby tells her with a wave as we hurry into the apartment. Bobby knows all the rich tenants. Then again, he knows just about everybody. "Excuse us," he says, "we gotta get our cat."

Mrs. Potter and the movers give us an amazed look as we hurry past them. One of the forms that Mrs. Potter is signing flutters to the floor. I pick it up and hand it back to her. *H.B. Moving Company* reads the letterhead.

"Hi, Pete," Charlie says to the short muscle-bound mover. But Pete doesn't turn to look at him.

And then I see the greatest sight I've seen all day. Fluffy's meowing at the fire-escape window.

Bobby yanks up the window. I grab the cat. And then Bobby, Charlie, and I all shout in triumph.

We won! We did it! We got Fluffy!

We take turns kissing her. She doesn't even seem

to mind, which is rare for a cat. Maybe she understands how close we all came to dying.

"She went out the window," I explain to Mrs. Potter and the movers, when I see them looking at us.

Suddenly Mrs. Potter lowers her head and starts crying.

"I'm sorry," she tells me. "It's just . . . hard for me, saying good-bye to this place, you know."

"She's retiring and moving to Florida," Bobby whispers to us as Mrs. Potter cries harder.

"Don't worry," Pete the mover tells her, patting her back. "We'll take good care of your stuff, believe me."

Maybe Pete's not so bad after all.

"You know what I tell my customers?" Pete goes on. "I tell them, just get out quick. You know, don't look back."

And don't look down, I think, giggling.

I know it looks like I'm laughing at Mrs. Potter, but I can't help it. I'm too happy.

Mrs. Potter, still crying, nods at Pete, mumbles a thank you, takes one last look around, then hurries out the door. The movers start for the door as well. All except Pete, who's staring at me for some reason.

"C'mon, Ray," one of the other movers calls to—

To Pete?

And then all of a sudden all these names fly through my head one after another . . .

M&M Movers.

R&R Movers

HB Moving Company.

And a man named Pete who answers to the name Ray.

Three moving men.

And as Ray stares at me I can see by the look in his eyes that I'm right. And he knows it, too. He knows I just figured it out.

It's the robbers.

CHAPTER 26

THE OTHER TWO MOVERS GO OUT THE FRONT DOOR. But Ray stays right where he is, staring at me.

I feel like a deer caught in the headlights, and the headlights are his eyes.

"What are you looking at?" Ray asks me, sauntering over. "Huh?"

"Nothing," I say. I gulp.

"This is Pete," Charlie tells Bobby.

"Pete?" asks Bobby. "I thought his friends just called him Ray."

"Ray, Pete, what's the difference?" I ask. "Come on, let's get out of—"

Ray blocks my way. "Where do you think you're going?"

"Back to . . . my apartment."

"To do what?"

"To do nothing. I live there. C'mon guys, let's—"

But before I can even finish my sentence, Ray grabs me in a headlock.

CHAPTER 27

"**H**EY! LET HER GO!" YELLS CHARLIE, FLAILING AT Ray. But Ray grabs him with his other hand and lifts him roughly into the air. I can barely breathe, he's holding my head against his stomach so hard. Fluffy is squirming and hissing like crazy in between us.

"Okay, kids," Ray snarls, "you're coming with me." He starts dragging us toward the bedroom. "You, too, fatso," he tells Bobby, herding him ahead of us.

Bobby backs up a few feet, then charges.

"Death grip!" he shrieks, squeezing Ray around the middle.

We all go down in a heap. Fluffy gets away from me, hissing like crazy. And then Ray screams as Fluffy bites his hand. Fluffy races away. Ray starts to get to his feet but he falls again. "My ankle," he moans.

"Run!" I yell at Bobby and Charlie. Charlie starts to run. So do I. But then we both have to stop to help Bobby back to his feet.

And Ray is getting back to his feet, too.

We start running, but he limps after us, sucking on his hand where Fluffy bit him, coming hard.

"Hey, Ray, you coming or what?" calls a voice from out in the hallway as—

We fly out the front door with me in the lead.

Straight ahead of us stand the other two movers, who are waiting on the service elevator.

"Get them!" shouts Ray.

I turn right.

Don't ask me why I turn right. I'm not thinking too clearly. If I was thinking clearly, I would have turned left and we could have gotten on the regular elevator and been in the lobby with Fernando by now. But I turned right.

So now we're racing down the hallway with the two movers right behind us. Racing to our only means of escape.

My old friends. The stairs.

As we come through the door into the stairwell, I hear the movers thundering down the hall after us.

"We've got to get down to the lobby to Fernando!" I yell.

But even as I yell this I'm signaling wildly at Charlie and Bobby that we should go the other way. We should go up.

See, there's one little half flight of stairs that leads up from the fourteenth floor. That's where we go—up a few steps. Then I stop and crouch down, waving at Charlie and Bobby to do the same.

My trick works!

The first two movers race through the door to the stairwell and clatter down the steps without looking back.

Ray starts limping down the steps after them.

But then he stops.

Turns.

You know what?

Maybe it wasn't such a good trick after all.

'Cause Ray is looking right at us.

CHAPTER 28

THIS TIME I DON'T HAVE TO SAY RUN. WE ALL JUST go.

And now we're running UP, UP, UP the short flight of stairs.

Up ahead is a big battered metal door. We bang through it.

Bright sunlight blinds us.

We're running across this soft black tar.

Then I realize where we are.

We're on the roof.

Charlie, remember how you wanted to play Man on the Roof? Well don't ever say your older sister is no fun. Because looky here. You got your wish. One game of Man on the Roof, coming right up.

I don't know how it happened, but Charlie,

Bobby, and I are holding hands in a chain as we run.

Ray is right behind us.

I've never run this fast. We're just about flying over the tar.

So when we come to the edge of the roof, we couldn't even stop if we wanted to.

We jump right off the roof.

CHAPTER 29

WE'RE NOT TOTALLY CRAZY. THE ROOF OF THE NEXT building is like a foot down and only a couple of feet away. We all make it no prob.

So does Ray.

I hear his footsteps right behind us, feel his fingers swiping at the back of my shirt. Hear him grunting and groaning and yelling at us and—

We keep running. Running. No time to think. No time to plan.

And as we run flat out across this roof, I see a very strange sight.

On the next roof.

On Hamilton House.

There's a man standing on the edge of the roof. A man with gray suit pants and a white shirt and a blue tie. Near the man—but not too close—are all these cops and firemen. Looks like they're all talking to the guy.

Which is when I remember. I remember this whole other crisis that's been going on right next to ours. The man on the roof!

"We gotta jump one more roof!" I yell to Bobby and Charlie as we run.

'Cause if we get over to Hamilton House we'll have all the cops on our side.

We're not holding hands anymore. But we all jump at the same time.

So we all see it at the same time.

You see—this next roof isn't nearly as close as the first one was.

The gap is too wide.

Which means—

We're all going to die.

CHAPTER 30

BOBBY FALLS ONTO THE ROOF OF THE NEXT BUILDING with a thud.

So does Charlie.

I'm the only one who doesn't make it.

I scream as I fall.

CHAPTER 31

But as I fall I latch onto the edge of the roof. I'm hanging by my fingertips!

I groan, trying to pull myself uppp. . . .

Can't.

Wow. Second time today. Only this time it's not a bookcase. This time it's the edge of a roof, fourteen stories high. And if I fall—

I stare at my hands, the knuckles bone white from the strain.

Suddenly my right hand slides off the tarry roof and—

I swing down fast and—

I can't hold on with just one hand, couldn't even hold on with two, and then—

My left hand starts to slide off the roof.

CHAPTER 32

FOUR HANDS GRAB MY WRIST.

Bobby and Charlie peer down over the edge of the roof. They pull me back up, up, up until—

I get my right hand back on the ledge. Now I can help them. As they pull I swing one leg up and over the edge and—

They pull me back up onto the roof, like they're pulling me out of the ocean.

We crawl away from the edge. Get to our feet. Bobby and Charlie hug me like crazy.

And here comes the man in the suit.

With tears in his eyes.

He hugs me, too.

It's Mr. Slocum. The jumper!

And then all the cops surround us.

"That's a robber!" I yell, pointing back at the next

roof, where Ray watches the whole scene, dumbstruck.

Ray turns and starts limping back the way he came. But the cops get on their walkie-talkies. And I blurt out the news about the moving van and the other two movers.

"Good work," the cops are telling us. "Good work!"

Everyone's slapping us on the back. The man in the suit is smiling and crying at the same time. He looks gray-faced and all worn-out. But happy, too. I notice the cops keep glancing at him, I guess trying to make sure he doesn't try to leap off the building.

I'm no psychologist, but I feel like Mr. Slocum is safe now.

I guess we saved him, too!

And right away I'm remembering what Mrs. Carmen said, about how he misses his three kids. So I hug him again. So does Charlie. So does Bobby. And we all just stand there crying. And then there's this huge cheer.

I can't believe it. It's a strange feeling. Like we're on TV. Then I get it. It's the crowd down in the street below.

I look down. People are throwing their hats in the air. Jumping up and down. Waving. It's like we just won the World Series.

There's only one little problem.

I'm looking down.

Fourteen stories.

At people the size of ants.

That can't be the old dizziness I'm feeling, can it?

Because I'm sure I just proved that I'm over my
fear of—
    Oh wow—
    The whole world spins fast around me and—
    I fall right off the building.

CHAPTER 33

A
Y
Y
Y
Y
Y
Y
Y
!
!
!
!
!
I—
hear—

this—
horrible—
scream—
from—
the—
crowd—
as—
I—
pick—
up—
speed—
end—
over—
end—
arms—
flying—
and—
oh—
wow—
fourteen—
stories—
is—
a—
long—
way—
to—

CHAPTER 34

Bam!!
!!

CHAPTER 35

YOU KNOW WHAT? I THINK I MUST HAVE HIT THE awning, 'cause I'm bouncing up, up, up, and—

Whoa! Now I'm falling again—

Only I'm not falling nearly as far as last time and—

BAM!

I hit this big blue thing again, and now I lie still. Facedown. Smelling vinyl.

But only for a second, because suddenly there are hands all over me, rolling me, lifting me, and—

I'm in this daze but—

There are cops and people in white uniforms with stethoscopes swinging from their necks and I'm being placed on a stretcher, only—

I sit up and start yelling. 'Cause I just realized

what I hit. The emergency trampoline. And I'm okay! I'm okay!

I peer up at the top of the building. When I see how far I just fell, I let out a horrible scream.

But there are so many sirens shrieking and people screaming and shoving and pushing and walkie-talkies blaring that I can barely hear myself. I get off my stretcher so fast I almost fall—

More hands reach for me but I scramble loose and keep running—

Until I get to the front door of Hamilton House. I wait there with the crowd surging toward me, and the reporters firing questions.

"I think she wants to try it again!" someone jokes.

I don't answer. Just stay right at the doors until finally—

Charlie, Bobby, and Mr. Slocum and the cops all come rushing off the elevator and run through the lobby to the front doors where I'm standing.

"I guess you guys took the slow way," I tell them with a grin.

And then Bobby and Charlie and I have another long group hug.

Flashbulbs pop. Or maybe my brain is exploding, I don't know. We're dancing. Jumping. But safe jumping for once. 'Cause hey—we're on the ground!

And then the reporters get their microphones in our faces. And I don't know what I'm saying. Only Bobby is able to make any kind of a speech. In fact, he goes on and on. All about how we're all heroes.

I shake Mr. Slocum's hand, pumping it up and down. And then the cops cut off the mini–press conference and take Mr. Slocum to an ambulance.

And some other cops push us kids through the crowd, escorting us to—

Where are they taking us?

All right! We're headed back to the Westholme.

Where the cops have already handcuffed the three movers. And where the real moving van is just arriving.

And there's Fernando, looking amazed, and there's Mrs. Potter, looking even more amazed. And there's Mrs. Carmen in her chair. . . .

Which is when it hits me.

Mrs. Carmen.

Mrs. Carmen knows what everybody in the building is up to, everyone says so.

Mrs. Carmen would know when the movers were supposed to come and what apartment to go to.

Mrs. Carmen would know when the painters were supposed to come, too.

Mrs. Carmen, who's too broke to pay last month's rent, but she's got an Aiwa CD player, cable TV, and today she's ordering a big-screen TV with cash on delivery.

And all the time I'm thinking this, Mrs. Carmen is watching me. And the way she's eyeing me . . . it's a lot like the look that was on Ray's face when he saw me figure out that he was a robber.

I shake my head slightly, to tell her that I won't turn her in. 'Cause for one thing, I have no proof. And for another thing, it's Mrs. Carmen.

Back in our apartment. Me and Charlie. Outside, the cops are arresting Mrs. Carmen. Turned out I didn't have to turn her in at all. Ray did it for me.

When they were shoving him in back of a cruiser he started yelling that the cops should arrest Mrs. Carmen, too.

What a great plan. Thanks to Mrs. Carmen, the robbers knew that Mrs. Potter was moving. So they arrived an hour early and packed up everything she had.

We'll take good care of your stuff for you, I remember Ray saying.

I'm sure they would have, too.

Anyway, I didn't want to watch the cops arrest Mrs. Carmen. And here's another thing I don't want to do. I don't want to leave this apartment until Mom comes home.

Charlie and I sit on opposite ends of the long ratty sofa in the living room, not saying a word.

We both stare at the TV.

The TV is off.

Who needs TV after what we just went through?

I don't know how long we sit here.

But then—

Charlie and I both turn our heads at the same time, staring at each other.

In horror.

And when we talk, we say the same word at once.

"Fluffy!"

CHAPTER 36

WE TAKE THE ELEVATOR. CHARLIE AND I BOTH KEEP
pressing the button for floor fourteen. Again and
again.

I don't like going up in the elevator, let me tell
you. I don't like seeing those little numbers lighting
up as we rise—

2, 3, 4 . . .

I liked being on the ground for once. I wanted to
stay right where we were—

8, 9, 10 . . .

The door to Penthouse C is wide open.

We race in.

Skid to a halt on the bare wooden floor.

The sound of Bobby's weeping echoes through the
vast empty apartment.

"Bobby!" I yell.

He lowers his hands from his chubby face. Then shakes his head slowly from side to side. "She jumped," he says. "Fluffy jumped. She's . . . dead."

CHAPTER 37

I'M NO DUMMY. YOU CAN FOOL ME TEN TIMES straight. But that's it.

So as soon as I hear the scratching sound coming from the closet, I realize it's all one of Bobby's dumb gags.

Unbelievable.

After all this.

I guess some people never change.

I stalk over to the closet and fling open the door. I scoop up Fluffy.

While Bobby just cackles hysterically.

But Charlie laughs along with Bobby. And I don't know. I guess I don't have any anger left in me. 'Cause I start laughing, too. And when Bobby asks if he can play with us and Fluffy, I even say okay.

Hey, I'm as surprised as you are.

And then we're all on the elevator, me, Charlie, Bobby, and Fluffy. Fluffy's squirming but I hold on tight, believe me.

"Charlie, do me a favor, would ya?" I ask. "Would ya tie your shoelaces?"

Charlie doesn't answer.

"Charlie," I say.

"It's the style," Bobby says. "Everyone's got them unlaced. All the cool kids."

"You be quiet," I tell him. He grins.

"Hey, Denise," says Charlie. "You gotta admit, at least you're over your fear of heights now, right?"

"Right," I tell him, smiling.

But I keep my eyes locked on the numbers of the floors as the elevator glides down. Down. I don't look away—not once—until we reach floor number one.

SUMMER '96... LIVE THE 3-D VIRTUAL ADVENTURE!

T2 TERMINATOR 2 3-D

UNIVERSAL STUDIOS FLORIDA®

For more information call (407) 363-8000 or visit our web site at http://www.usf.com